S0-BAC-773

The Bengal Tiger Boo-Boo

Based on the screenplay "The Wonder Pets Save the Bengal Tiger!"
by Billy Lopez and Josh Selig
Cover art by Little Airplane Productions
Interior illustrated by Kellee Riley

A GOLDEN BOOK • NEW YORK

Linny!

Tuck!

Wake up, Ming-Ming!

Will you connect the dots to finish this drawing for Linny?

Shoo, Fly!

The phone is ringing!

There's a beautiful Bengal tiger
with a thorn stuck in her paw!

This is serious!

Let's save the tiger!

Linny, Tuck, and Ming-Ming, too!

We're Wonder Pets and we'll help you!

Let's build the Flyboat!

That fly is causing trouble! We're big, important heroes with hero stuff to do! So shoo, Fly, shoo!

The marble for the mast is stuck inside this straw!

None of us can reach the marble!

Maybe the fly can help us! I bet he can fit
in the straw and get the marble out!

Can a small fly help the big Wonder Pets?

Whether you're big or small, live on land or in the sky,
all living things are important, even a fly!

Will you help the fly find its way through the straw to push out the marble?

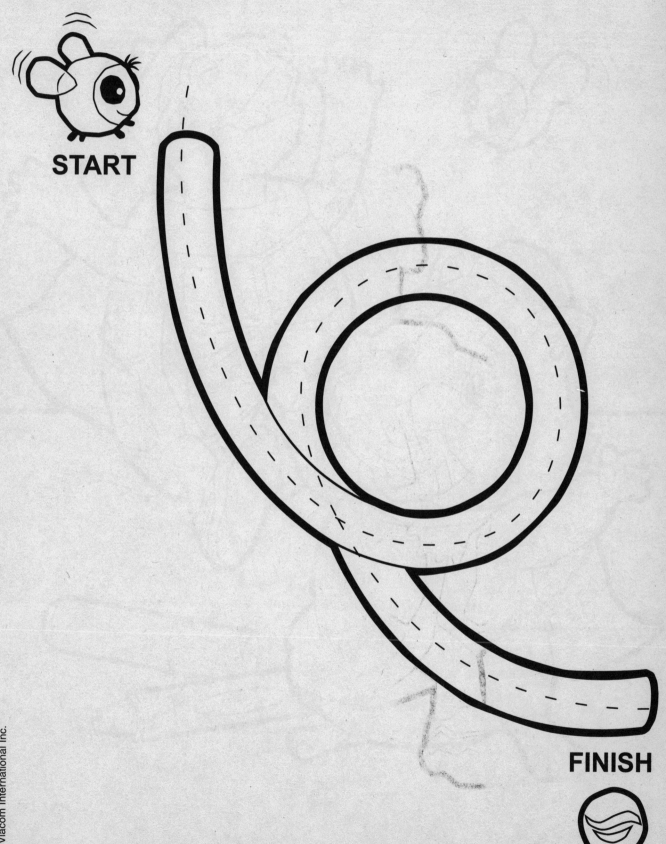

START

FINISH

Thank you, Fly! If you weren't so small,
we never could have gotten the marble.

I'm sorry I got angry, Fly.
You helped us get the marble out so we can save the day.

What's going to work? Teamwork!

Will you help the Wonder Pets by drawing a sail for the Flyboat?

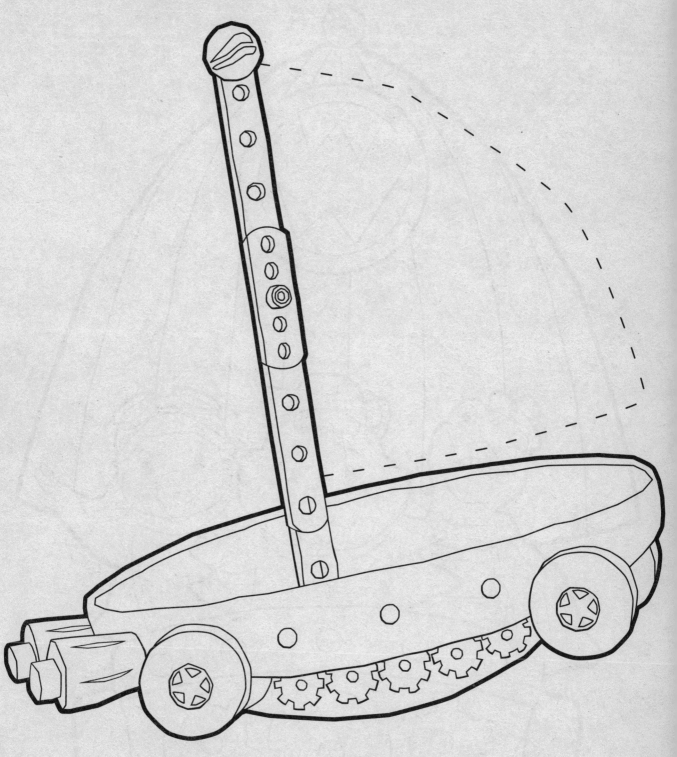

We're coming to save you, Bengal Tiger!

Will you help the Wonder Pets find their way to India?

START

FINISH

Look! It's the Taj Mahal. We're in India!

The Taj Mahal looks like a giant snow cone!

I see a cow! Do you? *Mooo!*

Let's land in this forest.

There's the tiger!

Her paw is hurt!

Your paw is in good hands . . .

. . . and wings!

So you've finally come, Wonder Pets.
Do you always take this long?

We got here as soon as we could, Bengal Tiger.

How did the thorn get stuck in your paw?

When I was picking flowers, just this very morn . . .

... I stepped on a rose with my tigery toes ...

. . . and got stuck by this thorn!

Will you use the key to color a rose for the tiger?
Watch out for the thorns.

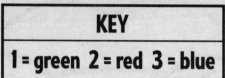

The thorn is stuck tight!

Wonder Pets, we need to pull this thorn out!

My hands are great for digging and holding celery,
but this thorn is too small for me to hold!

My hands are made for swimming and crawling, not pulling!

And I don't have hands, but I have heart! I'll do it!

My touch is as light as a feather—in fact, it *is* a feather!

Ooochee!

I haven't started yet!

Did someone say "thorn"?

I'm Raji, Puller of Thorns, known throughout the land!

If you need a thorn pulled out, I'm happy to lend a hand!

He's the best! He once pulled a thorn from my father's foot!

Raji has helped all kinds of animals—like this giraffe!

And this hyena, who made him laugh.

Will you help Raji get to the tiger?

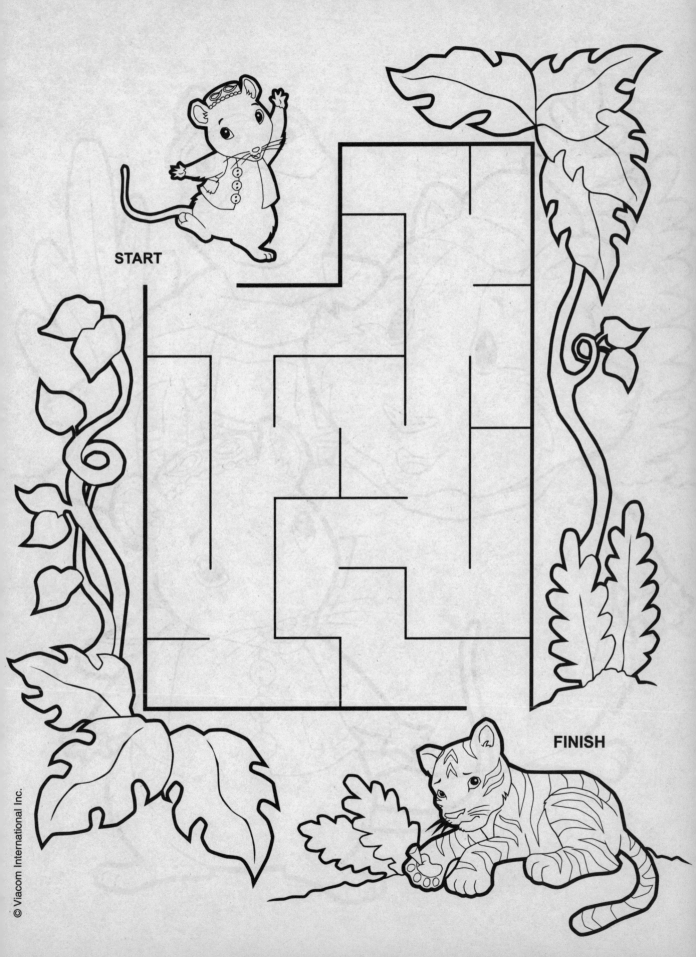

START

FINISH

Boy, are we glad you're here, Raji.

How could a small mouse
help a big Bengal tiger like me?

Will you draw a circle around the smallest animal and a square around the biggest?

I've pulled thorns from paws much bigger than yours!

I don't believe it!

Bengal Tiger, you shouldn't be so mean to other animals!

No matter how small they are.

Big or small, all living things are important!

Small animals can help big animals!

Sometimes an elephant can't reach
an itch he needs to scratch.

But a little crane can help him out.

I have been so foolish. The truth is plain to see:
Even a small animal can be as great as me!

I'm sorry I was mean. Please pull out the thorn.

Since you asked so nicely, I'll be happy to help.

I've got a good grip, but this thorn is just in too deep!

Farewell, my friends.
Raji, the once-great Puller of Thorns, is through!

Wonder Pets, we have to think of something!

We can work together!

Raji can pull the thorn, and we can pull Raji!

What's going to work? Teamwork!

Let's go for it!

Pull!

We got it! That's a keeper!

No more ooochee! No more boo-boo! Thank you!

It was our pleasure, Bengal Tiger!

This calls for some celery!

Celery? Never touch the stuff . . .

. . . unless it has curry on it!

Curry is a yummy spice from India.

Ooochee! That's hot! But I like it a lot!

Wonder Pets, I have learned
that small animals are important.

That's great, Bengal Tiger! We like being small!

These ladybugs also like being small.
Will you follow the key to color them?

KEY
1 = black 2 = red 3 = green 4 = blue

I like to flap my wings, but if they were any bigger,
I'd bump into things! I like being small!

Baby Elephant is smaller than his dad,
and he likes it that way.

Some of us are tiny! Some of us are tall!

But when we work together, there's room enough for all!

We found a way to help the Bengal tiger and save the day!
Goodbye!